DIEGO AND THE DINOSAURS

adapted by Lara Bergen
illustrated by Art Mawhinney

Ready-to-Read

SCHOLASTIC INC.

New York Toronto London Auckland Sydney
Mexico City New Delhi Hong Kong Buenos Aires

ISBN-13: 978-0-545-07607-4
ISBN-10: 0-545-07607-2

12 11 10 9 8 7 6 5 4 3 2 1   9 10 11 12 13/0

Printed in the U.S.A.

First Scholastic printing, January 2009

Hi, I am  !
DIEGO

Look! I am back in the

time of the DINOSAURS

for a rescue!

Do you like ?

So do we!

 lived a long, long time

ago.

Some  were big,
like this Brachiosaurus.

Some were small,
like this Microraptor.

This dinosaur is  .
MAIA

The [rain] washed away
RAIN

her family's   .
FOOTPRINTS

Now  cannot find them.

MAIA

 misses them a lot.

MAIA

I know!
I will use my
SPOTTING SCOPE
to find them.

Do you see 's family

MAIA

in my  ?

SPOTTING SCOPE

Yes! There they are.

They are on !

EGG   ISLAND

But wait!  is hungry.

MAIA

She is a plant eater.

She eats .

LEAVES

Do you see a

TREE

with lots of 🍃 ?

LEAVES

Yum!

Now we have to cross
the Rocky  cliffs.

ROCK

But look out!

There is a  slide!

ROCK

We need something soft to land on.

RESCUE PACK

can help us!

 here!

Are soft to land on?

No!

Is a soft to land on?

No!

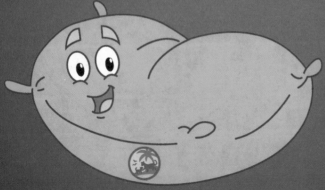

Is a big  soft to land on?

PILLOW

Yes!

Now we have to get
back up the  cliff.
ROCK
What can we climb?

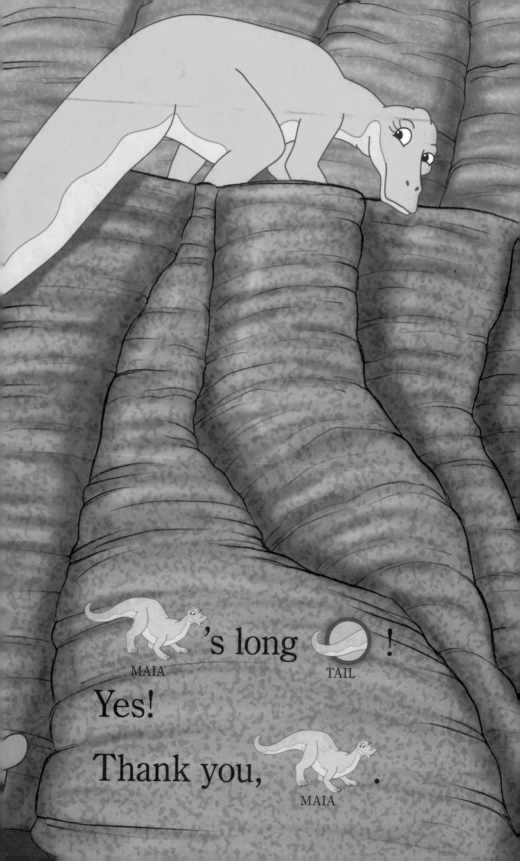

's long !

Yes!

Thank you, .

Now we can find your family.

But wait!  smells another .

MAIA

DINOSAUR

 MAIA stomps her big **FEET**

to scare them away.

Will you stomp your **FEET**

like a  **DINOSAUR** too?

Yay! There they go!

Look! There is  EGG ISLAND !
But how will we get
across the WATER ?

Did you know that lots of could swim?

DINOSAURS

Can you swim

like a too?

DINOSAUR

Hooray! We made it to

EGG   ISLAND !

And look!

There is 's family!

MAIA

Do you see their NEST

full of EGGS ?

We did it!

We helped  MAIA get home.